FROM
LETTER
TO
LETTER

FROM
LETTER
TO
LETTER

Teri Sloat

E. P. Dutton · New York

astronaut · airplane · acorn · apple · ant · alphabet · alligator · armadillo · ark · anchor · anthill ·

balloon · bluebird · butterfly · button · baby · block · bucket · bubble · bean · blossom · bee · bear ·

Look at the back of the book for more words for the pictures.

cherry · crayon · candy cane · cupcake · candle · castle · Christmas cookie · camel · clown · carrot ·

dinosaur · doll · drum · drumstick · domino · dice · deer · dog · daffodil · daisy · dolphin · dandelion ·

elephant · eight · eleven · eighteen · echidna · eagle · egg · eye · eggplant · ermine · Eskimo · elf ·

flag · fruit · flashlight · forest · fox · flamingo · frog · fish · fly · fiddler · fiddle · flute · farmer · flower ·

goldfish · grasshopper · gumball · gorilla · goat · goose · garden · gopher · gumdrop · gingerbread ·

hen · hive · honeybee · hat · hydrant · hopscotch · hose · holly · hamburger · hedgehog · hippopotamus ·

ice-cream cone · ice cube · iron · ironing board · inchworm · inch · impala · iguana · ink bottle · ink

jet · jack · joker · jump rope · jack-o'-lantern · jelly bean · jewelry · jack-in-the-box · jacks · jellyfish ·

kite · koala · kitten · knot · keyboard · key · keyhole · kid · kangaroo · kiwi · karate · kick · kung fu ·

lighthouse · lobster · lollipop · loon · lily · lion · lemon · ladder · library · librarian · light · leak · lock ·

moon · mountain · match · music · marble · mouse · mushroom · mole · magician · magic wand · mop ·

nuthatch · nest · nut · nail · nothing · notebook · needle · narwhal · nutcracker · newspaper · needlework ·

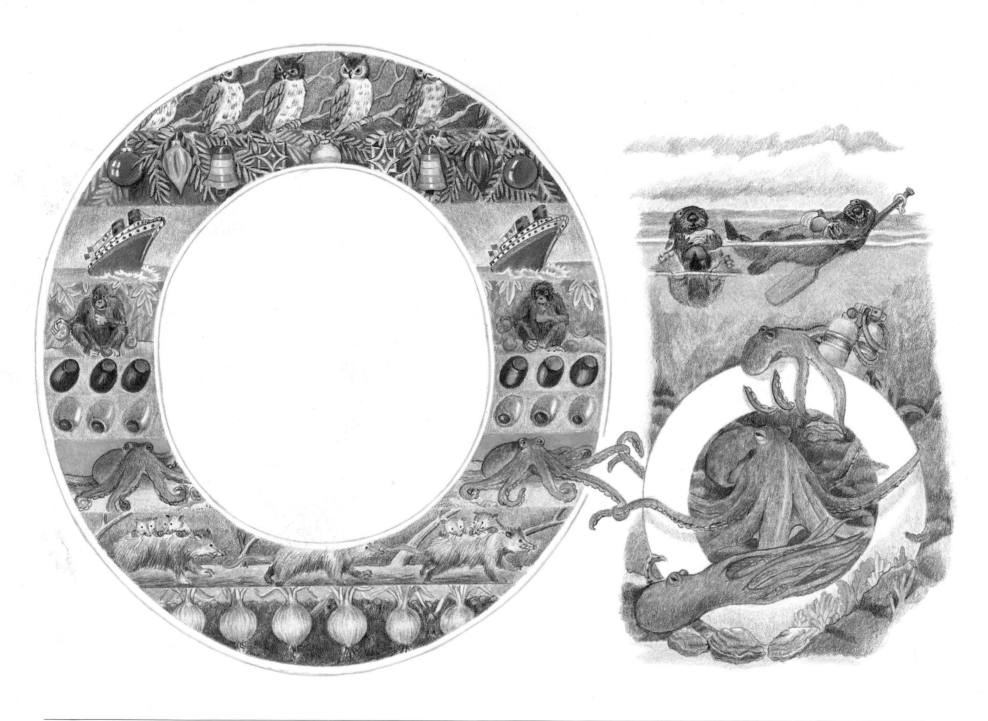

owl · ornament · ocean liner · orangutan · olive · octopus · opossum · onion · ocean · otter · oar

pear · peach · pig · penguin · pea · porcupine · paint · popcorn · pumpkin · parade · paddle · people ·

Quonset hut · quadruplet · quill · quail · question · quince · queue · quilt · queen · quicksand · quetzal ·

rainbow · rain · robin · raccoon · rat · rope · ring · ribbon · rose · rabbit · radish · rodent · race ·

satellite · space · squirrel · seal · stripe · stitch · star · skunk · strawberry · snail · swan · sand castle ·

train · traveler · tapir · toothpaste · toothbrush · toucan · tulip · tomato · tortoise · track · toy · town · tent ·

unicorn · uniform · underwear · umbrella · up · unicycle · utensil · ukulele · underpass · upside down ·

volcano · vulture · valentine · village · volleyball · vitamin · viper · vine · vicuna · violet · vendor · vest ·

windmill · woodpecker · wishing well · window · web · watch · wagon · wood · walrus · whale · wedding ·

x marks the spot · railroad X-ing · x means kiss · X ray · x wins tic-tac-toe · xylophone · extra large ·

yellow · yo-yo · yarn · yacht · yoke · yellow jacket · yucca · yam · yurt · yak · yard · youngster · yawn ·

zeppelin · zither · zebra zone · zipper · zigzag · zebu · ziggurat · zinnia · zucchini · zebra · zzzzz ·

A B C D E F G H I J K L M N

anteater	embroidery	goose girl	heart	jade
antennae	eyelet	garbage	head	juggler
air	earring	garbage cans	hook	jar
	Easter egg	gnats	hut	jam
birdhouse	edelweiss	grain	hedge	jelly
beak	egret	gate	haystack	jester
buttonhole	easel	glove	hydrangea	jawbreaker
bush		grass	hollyhock	jigsaw puzzle
blackberry	fur	gingham	hyacinth	jug
	fin	goblet	hummingbird	
caravan	fireworks	glasses	heather	knitting
cannon	finger	grapefruit	hair	knothole
cactus	field	ground	hand	kimono
cowboy	farm	gravel	hermit	
circus	food	graph paper	hill	lake
	friend			lime
dust	fence		island	lamppost
dots	fern		iceberg	letter
darkness			ice skater	lamb
dachshund			igloo	leaf
dirt			iris	lightning
			ivy	lizard
			ice pick	lace
				ladybug

a b c d e f g h i j k l m n

O P Q R S T U V W X Y Z

microphone	pod	Saturn	tepee	wash
moth	purple	snow	tunnel	wallpaper
medal	pink	seam	tree	wrist
mustache	puddle	sand	tower	wizard
	police officer	shovel	totem pole	witch
nestling	plaid	spoon	telephone pole	warthog
night	pigtail	scoop	tanker car	woods
notch	ponytail	shell	tender car	waterfall
name	pom-pom	sand dollar	trestle	winter
number	parka	sunglasses	trademark	wart
necklace	pennant	starfish		worm
nightlight	photo	sandpiper		
nickel	pin	sailboat	Ursa Major	
		surf	Ursa Minor	x-stitch
oxygen	quarters	sunset		
orange	Queen Anne's lace	seashore	villain	yardstick
oyster	quagmire		vegetable	yardage
			vase	
	racetrack			zero
	runner			zoom lens
	rag			zoologist
	railing			

o p q r s t u v w x y z

with thanks to Matt and Carrie

Published in the United States by
E. P. Dutton, New York, N.Y.,
a division of NAL Penguin Inc.

Published simultaneously in Canada by
Fitzhenry & Whiteside Limited, Toronto

Designer: Barbara Powderly
Printed in Hong Kong by South China Printing Co.
First Edition   10 9 8 7 6 5 4 3 2 1

Library of Congress Cataloging-in-Publication Data
Sloat, Teri.
    From letter to letter / Teri Sloat.—1st ed.
      p. cm.
    ''Published simultaneously in Canada by Fitzhenry & Whiteside,
Limited, Toronto''—Verso of t.p.
    Summary: Each page features a letter of the alphabet, drawn as
both a capital and a lowercase letter, decorated with pictures
of objects beginning with that letter.
    ISBN 0-525-44518-8
    1. English language—Alphabet—Juvenile literature.
2. Vocabulary—Juvenile literature.   [1. Alphabet.]   I. Title.
PE1155.S57   1989   89-1135
[E]—dc19   CIP
                                                AC